Where is Jasper?

"The Dearest in the Forest"

by

Andrea Burke

Hosur,
Tamil Nadu,
India

Email:
and_freelance@yahoo.com

BLUEROSE PUBLISHERS
India | U.K.

BlueRose ONE
Stories Matter
NewDelhi • London

For permissions requests or inquiries regarding this publication, please contact:

BLUEROSE PUBLISHERS
www.BlueRoseONE.com
info@bluerosepublishers.com
+91 8882 898 898
+4407342408967

ISBN: 978-93-6452-259-5

First Edition: March 2025

A memorable trip..

Fore word

As a part-time teacher, I had never dreamt of writing a book. I include reading and writing as a part of my healthy routine. Recently, I've published my poem books <Truda's Simple Doses> and <Truda's Double Dose>.

In addition to these achievements, I'm elated to publish my third book." The DEAREST IN THE FOREST" is a wonderful and impressive picture-illustrated short story. It's about a young boy <Jasper> who travels with his parents and sister. Their well-dressed smile is what one could imagine.

The writing is impossible to ignore. The family begins their trip to the forest. Unexpectedly, the boy falls out of the car while driving tumbles down from a peak, and is lost in the forest. The sense of the mystery and wonder within the forest is compelling and intriguing. The forest serves as a metaphor for deeper themes like human resilience or the unknown.........

Jasper who is mute(one who cannot speak) yet hearing embarks on a journey to find his way back to his family. Meanwhile, he encounters cute animals in the wild, and he feels like paradise in the wild. Do you know why? The story includes suspenseful elements and has an happy ending.

See you soon,
Sally!
Bon voyage,
Jasper!

I'm excited! This is incredible!
I feel loved and I am happy to be with
my family. I love this trip.

Jasper can only scream. His voice echoes
through and through the branches.
He imagines that there are shadows whispering
secrets that only the darkness will hear.

Scarlet Screams " Jasper"...
There were screams for help. Tears streamed down his face as screams echoed.

I'm slipping! I'm rolling! I'm tumbling down!
Help me, Mom and Dad. I can't hear any of you.
"Ow, Ouch!" My left hand hurts terribly.
This hole is pitch-dark. This silence numbs me.
I've fallen in here.

Suddenly, I see a glow with a hissing sound. It is startling. I find something creeping, slithering in the corner.

Oh, wow! She is smooth and glossy. Her iridescent sheen is beautiful. It seems that she has swallowed a prey. However, she gracefully wraps around her clutch of eggs. She has no feet to lift her body so she rests. I have to remain calm and not provoke her.

I wish I could play with her. I name this rainbow snake "Slinky". She seems like a caring mother. Oh No... I shouldn't become her Prey. I have to dart out quickly.

What do I do now?
How do I find my missing
loved ones?

Um.. I choose the trail on
my right while looking for
a signal on my watch.
I feel lost and Petrified.
I'm a lone wolf.

The branches look like gnarled hands reaching out to grab me. I have no idea where to go yet I have to keep moving.

The scent of the forest fills the air. It reminds me of my friend's mild perfume which makes me feel alive.

The leaves rustle in the wind, and the wind whistles through the branches. The light plays with shadows and colors between my fingers, calming my heart.

How soothing!

There are many wanderers: big, small, winged, furry, creeping, crawling, frightening ones around me.

Bees busily buzz. Cicadas and crickets

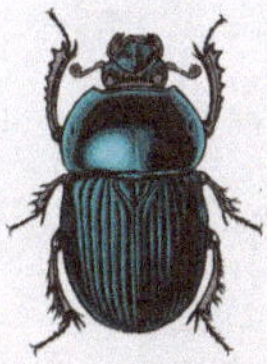

All of a sudden, I hear a noise in my stomach. I feel as hungry as a wolf. I'm worn out. Dad's reminder to fill my bag with essentials echoes in my mind. I always love croissants, I remember filling my bag with some croissants. I nibble on it to assuage my hunger. Yum! Yum!

Then, I notice a Bohemian Waxwing bird catching insects mid-air and soon it sits on a branch of the birch tree.

As I find her tail wagging, I softly, soothingly chirp, and then she drops a small stalk of berries near me. I relish its sweetness.

As soon as I settle down between the buttress roots, I observe the butterflies fluttering together towards me. Their wings caress my cheeks and tickle my ears. I feel tender and warmly comforted.

(Jasper has forty wings)

I startle on feeling the tremors. I can hear the distant trumpet sound of the elephants.

At the same time, I felt my bag moving away from me but I didn't find anyone around me.

Each second twitches my nerves and I feel petrified.

I scoot into a nearby cave tree to hide. I peek to admire a herd of elephants passing by. I observe the small calf between the herd that boldly strolls along them.

It makes me understand that I should navigate this huge forest.

After a while, I follow the elephant's trail.

Here again, I hear the growling sound. Is it a wolf? My mind feels like a whirlwind.

I rush to grab a sturdy branch that has broken off from a tree. I grabbed it swiftly and placed it by the tree to climb up gradually.

I secure my feet into the bark holes and reach out to its branch. I, then, silently lodge myself on the branch despite my fear of heights.

At dusk, the cool breeze makes me feel cozy. I admire the forest view.

From the swaying of trees to the twinkling of bright stars like diamonds calmed my mind.

The pale crescent moon flashes light throughout my night. I look around to sense danger while being entertained by the fireflies glowing, flashing their light, and dancing.

I peep down at the porcupines whining and moaning while their young ones play. It amuses me.

Ah!

The monster caught me!

Unexpectedly, without any noise, this eight-eye insect creeps downwards and looks directly into my eyes. I fall behind because it is scary. It jumps onto its spun silk web.

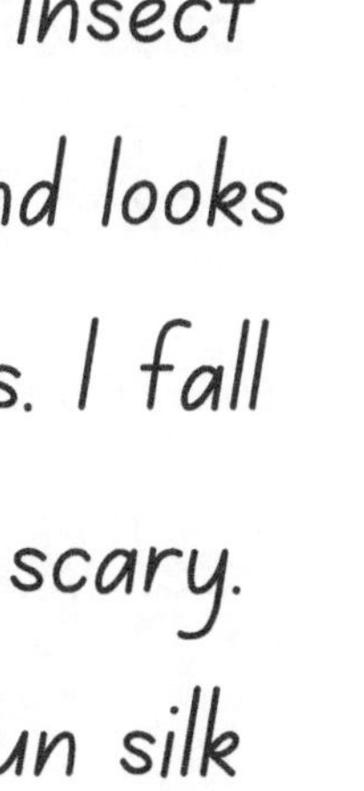

When I bend to withdraw my bag from the small branch, I feel something holding my hand tight. I didn't realize I was next to its furry body because it blended with the bar. Its claws grip the branches. It is lazy to move. It seems that he has been sleeping for hours. The lazy one makes me feel like heaven and I fall asleep beside it.

It is an owl that spreads its wings like a blanket keeping me safe and peaceful.

My night passes quickly until I hear a sweet song of a robin. It cheers my early dawn, and I play on my ocarina simultaneously.

I wander through the forest while playing on my ocarina wishing that my melodies reach my family.

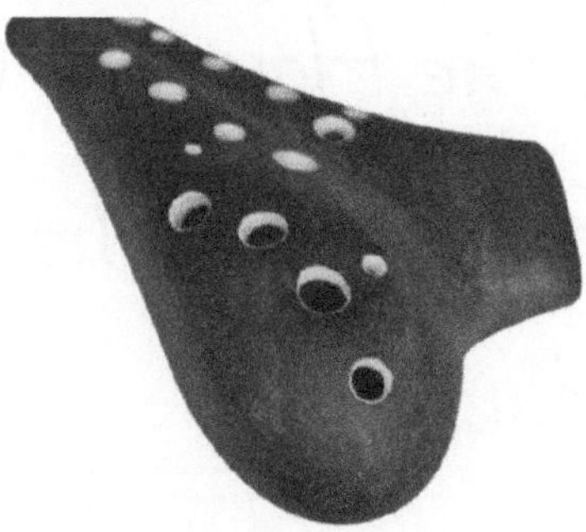

My eyes catch a beautiful cascade. The pristine flow of water is striking and I love to swim. So I cross over a few rocks to wet my legs but the slimy, slippery rock causes my fall. I slip and plunge into the water.

I swim along the Flounder, Carp, and Beta. Finally, I reached the other side.

I search for my bag at every nook and cranny. There!
I caught sight of it on a tree. It is a naughty monkey that has it. I found another one with my shirt on.

The other with my fedora on its head. They were swaying from tree to tree. I tried hard to climb and to reach them.

When I almost grab my bag, a packet of croissants falls out. The monkeys start fighting aggressively for food. I take off my belt to tackle the situation. I, then, slide to the other branch.

I didn't expect an old monkey to give me a blow from behind.

I stumble over my feet and fall off the shaky branch. I become as scared as a mouse in a cat's lair.

I faint before I drop to the ground. Suddenly, I feel that I am wrapped around to be coiled gently. It is "Slinky! "

She looks into my eyes as if I'm her Prey. Unexpectedly, it slithers swiftly to a cliff.

Upon hearing a helicopter sound, she rolls me down near the cliff.

I slip my hands into the pocket and pull out my torch. I flash the purple light towards the direction of the helicopter.

In a while, the crew spots me and extends a rope to pull me up.

A cheetah suddenly leaps to attack me. Quickly, I'm pulled up. I shrill in panic and then the word "Dad" is uttered.

Gleefully, I articulate (he begins to speak)

Yay!

On seeing my Dad, I burst into tears and hugged him. The crew offers immediate help. We reach our destination and I'm overjoyed to call out. I meet my mom and my sister "Scarlet". They are surprised to hear me speak.

Unexpectedly, I realized that my sister didn't respond. I feel sad that she lost her hearing in panic when the car tumbled down the road.

Our Story

Despite all these unforeseen events, we are grateful for reuniting. Our bond will last forever.

Do you know what animals I met?

You can face any situation with confidence.